Surprise Par for Mom

by Anne Giulieri

illustrated by Susy Boyer

"Alex," said Dad.
"Where is Mom?"

"She is in bed," said Alex.

"I can cook pancakes for Mom.

It is a **big** surprise!"

"I can cook
the pancakes, too," said Dad.

Dad and Alex
cooked the pancakes.

"Mom can eat this pancake,"
said Dad.

"She can eat this banana, too,"
said Alex.

"It can go on the pancake."

"Oh, no!" said Alex.

"Where is Mom?

She is not in bed."

"Alex," said Mom. "Where are you?"

Alex jumped up!
Dad jumped up, too!

"Surprise!" shouted Alex.

"Surprise!" shouted Dad.

"Here is a surprise pancake for you," said Alex.